This book belongs to:

_____

Published by Ladybird Books Ltd
80 Strand London WC2R 0RL
A Penguin Company
13 15 17 19 20 18 16 14

Printed in Italy

Sly Fox and
Red Hen

illustrated by Peter Stevenson

Red Hen lived in a
little house in a tree.

4

Sly Fox lived in the wood.
And he was hungry.

Sly Fox picked up his black bag.

"I'm going to catch Red Hen and eat her," he said.

Sly Fox hid in Red Hen's little house.

"I'm the Fox, I'm the Fox, I'm really sly. You can't beat me, however you try!" said Sly Fox.

Red Hen saw Sly Fox
and jumped up out of
his way.

"You're the Fox, you're
the Fox, you're really sly.
But you won't catch me,
however you try!" said
Red Hen.

"I will catch you," said
Sly Fox, and he ran
round and round
and round.

Red Hen's head went
round and round, too.
She fell down into
Sly Fox's big black bag.

Sly Fox ran into the
wood. The big black bag
was heavy, and Sly Fox
sat down to rest. Then he
fell asleep.

Red Hen jumped out of the bag.

"You're the Fox, you're the Fox, you're really sly. But you won't catch me, however you try!" said Red Hen.

21

Red Hen put some
heavy stones in the bag.
Then she ran all the
way home.

Sly Fox tipped the bag into the cooking pot.

"I'm the Fox, I'm the Fox, I'm really sly. I will eat you. Say goodbye!"

24

The stones fell **splash!** into the hot water.

"Ouch!" said Sly Fox. "I really hate that hen!"

26

Read It Yourself is a series of graded readers designed to give young children a confident and successful start to reading.

Level 2 is for children who are familiar with some simple words and can read short sentences. Each story in this level contains frequently repeated phrases which help children to read more fluently. Every page in the story is accompanied by a detailed illustration of the main action, which aids understanding of the text and encourages interest and enjoyment.

About this book

The story is told in a way which uses regular repetition of the main words and phrases. This enables children to recognise the words more and more easily as they progress through the book. An adult can help them to do this by pointing at the first letter of each word, and sometimes making the sound that the letter makes. Children will probably ı less help as the story progresses.

Beginner readers need plenty of help and encouragement.